Approaching Zero

Approaching Zero

Also by Roland Leach
Shorelines
drowning ophelia
My Father's Pigs
Obliquity

Roland Leach

Approaching Zero

Acknowledgements

These short stories and flash fiction have been published in *Antipodes* (US), *Apeiron Review* (US), *Crow, Famous Reporter, Fish Anthology 2021* (UK), *Indigo, Island, Mascara Literary Journal, Newcastle Short Story Anthology* 2018, *Newcastle Short Story Anthology* 2019, *Newcastle Short Story Anthology* 2020, *Oblong* (UK), *Scatterlings of Empire* (Journal of Australian Studies, UQP), *The Best Small Fictions 2015* (Queens Ferry Press, US), *The Weekend Australian, Westerly* and *Wet Ink.*

Approaching Zero
ISBN 978 1 76109 458 3
Copyright © text Roland Leach 2023
Cover image: Kim Maple

First published 2023 by
GINNINDERRA PRESS
PO Box 3461 Port Adelaide 5015
www.ginninderrapress.com.au

Contents

Desert

She left before dawn could throw its lit sacrament on morning alleys and wandered quietly back to her sequestered life behind wooden gates. He searched cobbled streets, the small bar where they had met asking for the short-haired girl. Began to believe that he imagined it all, conjured a silk dream. Then not an email or text, twitter nor a tweak, but an old postcard:

It is best to get
Indoors before the dust storm
Brings back the desert

Night

Margaret lay on her side, niggling down a little so she wasn't leaning too hard on her hip. She had been without her husband five years, seven if you counted his last two years in a nursing home. Her beloved German Shepherd died a month ago. If she had to choose between having her husband or dog alive again she would have her dog, Mardie, back.

But this night she was feeling vulnerable. She was getting old she thought, really old. Crumpled, wrinkled, decaying, decrepit, old. She wished that she still smoked. She would like to get up and make a cup of tea and have a cigarette; she wished she had her dog to pat, to rub her head into the ruff of fur around his neck. She could almost cry. She hated being old, this old. Things died and disappeared too quickly.

It was one a.m. She heard the sound of the old rusted muffler, the ragged exhaust that belonged to some old V8. She could tell the driver was trying not to press down too hard on the accelerator.

Nobody in this suburb drove cars like that. They were BMWs, Mercedes, Audis, prestige four-wheel drives. All had perfect exhaust systems. She was told by Peter, a few houses up the street, that gangs sometimes roamed the suburbs at night. A driver dropped off different members, then came back and picked them up along the streets. They would break into homes and cars, taking anything valuable.

She thought of her husband for the first time for many

months, it might have been years. Despite the emptiness of their marriage, the fighting and unhappiness, she never felt scared when he was in the house. He would have been able to take care of any intruder.

She remembered fondly his arms. They were tanned and rose like mountain swells. The thought surprised her.

She thought she heard the car stop. She didn't want to get up and look out the window. Her body would ache and it would take her ages to get comfortable again. But there was silence now where there had been the slow, husky roll of an exhaust with a hole in it.

No, I am not moving she told herself. She tried thinking of the ocean, closing her eyes and breathing in deeply and slowly, trying to imagine the breath of air moving within her.

The noise of the car started again. He had not turned off the car, just stopped. The hollow sound of the exhaust was there. The Saint Bernard across the road gave two quick yelps as though he was uncertain if he had heard a noise or not.

I am growing into the stereotype of an old defenceless woman. I will not let it happen, I will not. She thought of getting up and opening the front door, leaving it open for someone to come in and then if someone appeared, to ask them if they would like a cuppa tea, a piece of carrot cake. They would have a great old talk and she might even tell them to rob Jack Ramsay up the road in 41. He was such an old bastard he deserved it.

But she didn't. She lay back and tried to sleep.

She heard the click of the metal gate open. It was hard and distinct, a sound you couldn't mistake. She was standing on her feet and surprised herself how quickly she had moved. She did not even feel the muscles move as she would normally in any movement. She looked through the window but the gate was hidden behind a hibiscus. It was a clear night with a light breeze. Perhaps she had not closed shut the metal lock properly and it had blown open. She moved into the other room to look out of the window. Nothing.

She turned on the lights in the house and sat in her chair. Perhaps she should move into one of those homes or villages her daughters have been promoting since their father's death. There would be people around all the time, she might even make friends. She would never be scared like she was now. She had always been able to fend off her daughters as nearly all of these places didn't allow dogs. Maybe now she had to give in.

She hated giving in. She hated being scared, hated this body, this self she had grown into.

It didn't seem that long ago that she was a young girl flirting with boys. Spending all that time dressing up in front of mirrors and imagining the future. The dances during the war were like nothing else. She had fallen madly in love with a young pilot who could dance like Astaire; she could still feel his arms around her if she tried. But it was wartime and he flew off and she had married someone more earthbound.

Those summer nights walking home she loved the best. It didn't feel as if it was sixty years ago. Then her three daughters growing up. They were wonderful as babies. She would have liked to have preserved them in their pre-teen years but they grew up. The eldest in her fifties. She had looked in the mirror one day and there was a young girl staring back, now she refused to look, or only glanced sideways in case she had lipstick over her face.

No, she would not become this scared old woman, she refused. What's the point? I am nearly dead anyway, why fret over what can happen to me? She was going to buy a packet of cigarettes first thing in the morning. Fuck them, she thought and the words in her mind made her laugh. They made her sound a younger Margaret, one who wouldn't be huddling in her lounge room fearful of the world outside.

Her head flashed sideways. Did she see someone move amongst the clothes on the line? Fear filled her again, but this time she controlled it. I am an old woman, I have nothing to lose; I have already lost everything.

She opened the back door and looked out. She didn't say anything for a minute, but then it came out, a voice she noticed immediately as one she had lost many years ago: playful and ironic, but also defiant.

'Hello, anyone out there?'

A pause.

'You wouldn't have a cigarette, would you?'

She waited. The night air felt liberating.

Back inside, she moved with what seemed greater purpose, a quicker step. She went back to bed.

The metal click of the gate. One opening, another closing.

Good, she thought. She thought about her dog. She had loved him so much but she didn't need to have something that was loyal and dependent, nor did she want to be dependent. She would ring the Cat Haven tomorrow. She would get a cat. She would learn from it.

Deatth.com

It was a bright and cloudless morning, still cool but intimating that it would be warm by noon; the sort of day that friends of Raymond's would say, 'You wouldn't be dead for quids.' It was the day Raymond turned seventy two.

He left his house, walked down the purple street of jacaranda in bloom, and thought it couldn't happen today. He drew in a deep breath and the smell, the light shade of blue sky, reminded him when he was seventeen. The summer after he finished school. He came over the hill and saw the ocean and wondered how many times his heart had risen on seeing the colour of ocean blue.

He had between a minute and 1,095 days left to live, or it might be 365 days. He didn't know for sure.

Ten years before on his sixty-second birthday he had contacted DEATTH, an organisation that kindly organised a specialised brand of euthanasia. They knew many wished for death but often changed their minds or lost them as they grew too old. They arranged a client's death five to ten years in advance. The clarity of one's life could often be lost when faculties started to wane so they devised a contract whereby all responsibility would be taken from the client once they gave permission. Their death could occur on any day in the nominated year. Death at shorter notice could be negotiated when a client was obviously suffering but they were a group who filled a special niche market and once a person had been legitimately taken to hospital they refused to intervene.

Raymond was not a particularly sad or morbid man, but he had seen old age and refused to endure it. DEATTH was an organisation with the specific philosophy that catered for people who found old age undignified and its endurance absurd. People had no say in their birth, little in their life, so DEATTH allowed them to be defiant in death. Allowed them to make at least one big decision before departing.

For Raymond, it was more personal than this. He had seen many wither away. His father stared at a television for the last five years of his life with dribbling white lizards of saliva down his chin, believing when he was conscious of others that he was still living in an earlier time. The nursing home was full of these stories. Life was reduced to looking forward to the next meal.

DEATTH saw itself as an ethical response to a changing world where life expectancy had increased significantly but many aspects of people's physical and mental capacities had not. They also offered a great range of deaths, including the spectacular and extreme.

People could meet death by being taken out to the main-break at Teahupo'o on a big day. Strapped to a surfboard, they would be towed into a massive wave. Their last vision of life heroic as the arching, aching body of wave, born from a shift in depth, a gradient pull that steeps the face, offered before them a long barrelling tube over shallow reef. This option was not taken up only by old surfers or those in love with the sea, many landlocked individuals, timid in life, had signed up for this watery death.

There was skydiving with chutes that never opened. One minute of total weightless freedom as the earth rushed up to meet you. There was mountain climbing, diving and a whole list of leisure and sporting deaths. But DEATTH didn't just accommodate the sporting finale, they were proud to offer in their catalogue an extensive list of deaths that remembered great cultural, political or intellectual moments in history.

Hemlock could be administered to your food, and dressed in flowing robe (extra for a shrewish woman still complaining in the background) you could face your end stoically in the philosopher's death. Lincoln's death was popular in the US, though because of poor theatre attendance it often reverted to a cinema, usually at a local multiplex. You could choose a famous painting – Goya's *The Third of May, 1808*, and the *Death of Marat* being favourites – and the staff of DEATTH would dress you in costume fitting the era and have specialists knife, garotte or execute you in a way deemed most authentic.

The most popular and cheapest death was the single-bullet assassin. Many of the other options necessitated some final compliance and willingness to go at the end. This was often not the case and the very thing that DEATTH was set up for: too many failed to accept death when it was to happen in the coming seconds. The bullet on the other hand could come at any time in the designated year and you would never know.

They also accepted deaths not in their catalogue but refused crucifixions.

There were those who made a contract and decided to cancel but DEATTH refused to communicate. They often tried to hide away, escape to end of the world locations but the group sought out these people, knowing it was exactly these people who needed them. Their last difficult client, Mary M, was assassinated on Easter Island by a sniper hiding behind a fallen moai while Mary looked out over the sea that stretched unhindered to Antarctica. People like this kept premiums high but DEATTH believed in their ethical, if not philanthropic, mission. They imagined a world where the aged and infirm did not have to sit out bored aimless or mindless days.

When Raymond turned seventy-one, he decided to contact DEATTH. He never wanted to get old, and doomed by genetics he refused to wither away like his father, but he now thought that seventy-two might have been an early call – he was fit, still enjoyed getting up every day, still got a look from certain women his own age. He would ask to put it back two years: he would die at seventy-four instead.

He never got a reply. He tried for a year; every day for 365 days. They must have realised it was not a whimsical request. Perhaps they made the change without acknowledgement; keeping in line with their strict policy not to make contact.

Today he turned seventy-two; he didn't know why they used the term 'turned', as if a birthday was a street corner, or a stone turned over to reveal…what? Or to be turned into something 'other', the unwitting recipient of an inevitable spell. Perhaps he had two more years, he didn't know. He thought that they would at least not kill him early in the year as his request suggested there was no rush.

He walked down the hill towards the beachfront. There was a new sculpture that had been situated on the edge of the path, looking over the beach, that he wanted to see. It was made of steel and circular in shape, but reminded him of a human head. He thought of the great moai heads on Easter Island with their backs to the ocean, looking eternally inwards. He thought of what was going through his ex-wife's head at this very moment; and his son who had always wanted children but it hadn't happened. He wished he had some idea about how people really thought. How they experienced the world. If their feelings and sensations were in any way similar to his own.

Raymond noticed a teenage boy carrying a surfboard walking up the pathway from the beach. If only he could be seventeen again, to have that assurance of movement. For a second, he thought that the boy looked like himself, was himself in fact, more than half a century ago. Even from a distance there seemed something peaceful in the way the boy moved, an other-worldliness about him, like a reverent with the sacrament still wet on his mouth.

A minute later, the boy passed in front of the sculpture. He casually turned to Raymond, almost without seeming to move his head, and said, 'Cool' and moved on.

The bullet made a neat round, almost bloodless, hole in his forehead. A perfect shot by a skilled gunman. There was no pain, no suffering, no anxious waiting. It couldn't have been better. It was a gift.

Caves

She lived near the railway line on the leeside of older suburbs, with its turrets and wide balconies. I could never visit her at her parents' home, so it was left to her to arrange where we met. Occasionally it was in the gardens of the city but mostly it was at the beach.

I would wait at the bus stop, sitting on a low wall, my back to the ocean, tracing her passage down the aisle, watching for her to push back her hair as she came down the steps.

There was something wrong with her brother, they said. I didn't ask.

Some days I would be waiting and she wouldn't arrive. She had warned me about her father. I would wait for the next bus then go home. But when she did, we walked a thin trail through the rocky cliffs above the surf break till we came to the opening of a cave in the ground. I had been coming here for years with the guys. It was our secret place, though everyone knew about it, and we would smoke our first cigarettes. Now I brought her here, stepping down rock slabs to the cool darkness of a sand bottom and a hidden enclave.

From the path, it must have seemed we were descending into the underworld, eyes straight ahead, never looking back, finding in a familiar darkness, clefts of skin we wandered into.

There was one time she invited me, when her father was out, to meet her brother. She never mentioned her mother. At a first glimpse, he seemed like anyone's brother, perhaps too pretty, a pale Elvis. Only when I drew closer, I saw the white space in the heart of his eyes, the croaking sounds when he tried to speak.

It was just then that her father arrived home. I never saw such terror in a person's eyes as she pushed me out the back door and made me promise to stay there and be quiet till she came back.

It was behind the poinciana that I hid till she came back; now excited and scared at what she had risked.

Later she would tell me that her father would not let her out with boys: If they knew about your brother, there'd be no wanting you, bad stock, they wouldn't chance a son like that. So she had to wait till she was ready to marry, and when a man came along, they would finally have to put her brother away. Hide him away for good, in an institution. Her coming out meant his incarceration.

A few months later, we broke up. We were only seventeen after all. It was an early sign of the ease in which I could walk away without looking back.

Angle

I only knew an angle of my father. An acute angle. A tiny slice that changed from where you stood. I sometimes caught him in the corner of my eye and thought that's him. Getting out of his truck, dirty from work, pine resin on his arm hair, black oil across his face. Or in the Chrysler with the kids singing.

Never was.

I tried to look in the wrong direction, hoping he had left something of himself. Just a trace, so had I been a sniffer dog I could have tracked him.

But he was light-footed, shadowless.

He came home every day but was never there, came home every day with his one trick of disappearing into light.

Premonition

She gave birth inside a makeshift tent
beneath a broken moon, within a grove
of sheoaks, and though not a religious
woman, heard a voice that could
only have come from beyond.
She foresaw the lovelossdespair
to come. Knew she could double,
triple her size, grow claws,
tear any threat to then.
That there would be love everafter,
afterever and more,
yet would never be so loved.

Fathers

Fathers can be menacing figures. There is a palpable power in their silences. In their stares across the table. Even when they are smiling and saying, Good onya boys, as you are coming off the footy ground. They expect so much. Or nothing.

Mothers only expect too much.

Fathers' silences are different from the silence of mothers. Their whole look, the loose turn of the head, the relaxed movement of bone and muscle, the cut of their jib, all say, This is me. I am being what I am.

But there are unstated rules, unsaid things. There is a game you must learn and the first rule is knowing it isn't a game.

My mother asks me if I want a father; she will get me one if I want.

I think about it for a while. It would help in some situations, but I tell her that they sound too much like trouble.

She smiles and agrees. They are indeed, but I would have got you one if needed.

I wonder if I have made a mistake. I would have a father on the sidelines at the footy, like the other guys. My mother comes, of course, but she knows nothing about the game. The fathers sometimes slap you on the back when you come off the ground or rub your head and say, Great game, son. Or, You go in hard like a Trojan.

I just smile and say thanks, though I want to say, the Trojans lost.

All the footy fathers know my mum is the only female on the boundary line. They think she's all right and they often go over and say a few words about her 'little Barassi'. She tells me this later and laughs saying, What the hell is a Barassi? It sounds like a cross between women's underwear and a cocktail.

Still, I can tell when they compliment me they are thinking I should have a dad. I would be a better player if I had a dad.

I know that fathers cannot be judged by what they say on footy days. Fathers at football games are different from fathers at home, fathers at the pub, fathers at work. They are easy-going and casual at games. They joke and laugh. Their manner suggests that the world is wonderful and we shouldn't take it too seriously. They look as though they could fix any problems with a bit of light-hearted banter.

I like this about football. Whether there is jubilation over a win, or heads drooped with a loss, there is a sense of achievement, a bonding, a battle fought. Despite it being all about the number of times a ball goes between two white sticks, there's sweat and dirt, sore muscles, skinned knees and worse. It is a man's domain. We have a team song. We sing loudly and jump up and down. It is about boys with their fathers watching.

My mother says this is dangerous talk. You're too bright and educated to fall for those games and the narrative they embody, she says.

I tell her I know it's a game.

Despite reading far too many novels, I play harder than anyone else, and I am accepted. Still there is some suspicion, as if something is not quite right, as if something will come to light one day and show I am not quite like the rest. My mother will be blamed for this.

All fathers read newspapers. At the breakfast table they read the headlines, the business papers and the sports pages – some only read the sports pages. Fathers definitely don't read novels. Theirs is a world of facts and numbers; things that really happen. There is a solidity about fathers that comes from this. Their feet are planted firmly on the earth; there's cause and effect, and results that can be dealt with. There is a fluidity about novels, they are only stories, not good enough. They are unsatisfactory if you are going to deal with the things men must deal with.

I know some men must read because of all the English teachers and university professors in the world, but they may also be suspect. These men are more likely to question what is obviously common sense.

A father might teach me this.

My mother asks one more time if I want a father.

No, I say, too sternly. I don't. I don't.

Nightfish

'Can we go fishing tonight, Dad?'

The eleven-year-old boy had only been night fishing once. Walking along the high road above the beach seeing the fishermen's lamps; the darkness of the ocean that melted into sky, and then the white splash of the sinkered line hitting the water before disappearing. He had loved that night on the beach; just his Dad and him on the beach together, silent most times but it didn't matter. They got excited and let out hooting sounds when they thought they got a bite and he remembered the smile on his father's face when the first fish was landed. He had caught a tailor that night. A smaller one, not as big as his father's two. Silver. A night fish.

'Not tonight. Too windy.'

'But Dad, look outside, there's no wind.'

'There would be wind on the beach. Onshore wind. Another night.'

His father had promised all week that they would go fishing on Friday night. He stared out the window; there was no breeze. They were only three houses up from the beach. There was no wind, but he couldn't disagree with his father, who had already grabbed a bottle of beer from the fridge and had sat down in front of the television to watch the news. There would be no moving him now.

His mother came in. 'Another night, Michael. It is only the first week of summer. There will be months and months of hot weather and still nights.' But he didn't trust his father to ever take him again. The beach was a hundred yards away but his father would never take him back there.

His mother seeing his disappointment added, 'Lots of nights with fish jumping out of the water.'

He couldn't tell her that it was herring that jumped and boiled on the surface of the water. Tailor were a night fish that lived close to the bottom. They never jumped.

He went into his room and took out an atlas of the world. A large, green hardback with a circular vision of the earth embossed on the cover. He turned to the page with the map of Australia and the Indian Ocean stretching all the way to Africa. Thousands of miles of water in different shades of blue that signified depth. How many fish were there in that ocean? Fish being devoured at this very minute, others being born, small and seeing for the first time water that went forever. How many in those dark blue patches on the map, which lived in eternal darkness? Night lasted twenty-four hours a day. There wouldn't be day, he thought, at such depths. No light could ever penetrate that far down.

'Have a shower before dinner, Michael.'

He turned to the pages at the back of the atlas that had all the facts: the lengths of the longest rivers, the great mountains, seas and oceans. The deepest parts of the earth and sea. The Marianas Trench. Almost seven miles deep. It was further than the distance between Cottesloe and Scarborough. It would almost be as far as the City Beach groyne. All that way down in one of those underwater…what was the name of that thing… a bathyscape. All the way down in the bathyscape with it growing darker and darker. They would have great lights on the front to see. Great lights that would briefly light up a world that had only ever been coloured by darkness; it would be like the sun rising for the very first time. And beneath the sea there could be anything.

'Michael.'

At dinner he refused to look at his father. He looked down at his plate and slowly ate. He knew his father would not even mention fishing; wouldn't sympathise or promise next week.

It was only his mother who tried to make conversation. 'How was school, Michael?' Was he working on a school project? What mark did he get for his Oceans assignment? Where was his team playing football at the weekend?

He didn't look at his father but he imagined him sitting eating; his tanned face accentuated by his grey-white hair. Without any expression on his face, just bringing up food to his mouth. He was angry with his mother for still appearing happy, as if nothing had happened.

Back in his room he went back to his books. He had a small bookcase full of books on animals, the sea, dinosaurs. He had a theory that the Loch Ness monster was an ichythosaurus. They had long necks and lived in the water and could have survived the meteorites that supposedly killed the dinosaurs. He was going to prove this when he got older, or else be a marine biologist. But for the moment he was obsessed with how sea creatures deep beneath the sea lived in eternal darkness. His mother had told him many times that he had all the brains in the family. She would one day sit in the pews of the halls of a university and watch him walk up and collect his degrees, dressed in a black cape and wearing a mortarboard.

He grabbed the T volume of the *Encyclopaedia of Animals*

and looked up tailor. It wasn't there. There were tailor-birds, a type of warbler, but no tailor. Another certainty fell away from his world. Things changed too much. It was like the countries of Africa. His atlas had names of countries that were no longer there. Rhodesia and Congo had disappeared. It was like the beach in winter. Unrecognisable, with the sand washed away. At Trigg the sandbank that was crowded with surfers all summer was rocky and deep. At least the sand came back every year, but some things would never come back. He wanted permanence and the more he learnt, the more he felt as if he was travelling into a strange country; no, it was more like descending beneath the water where light diminished slowly till there was only darkness.

He closed his book. He heard his father close the bedroom door.

Outside was still, with not a breath of wind.

95 days

I am fifteen years old and with a bit of luck will be sixteen soon.

I live with my three sisters in an old house – my sisters say 'grand old house' – on the river. It is not ours of course. It belonged to the Strattan family, a rich old fifth-generation family. I only know this because of the things we have found in the house.

When we walked in, it seemed as though the family had just left. Everything in perfect order. There was ham in the fridge, though the milk was off. There were all the latest technologies and comfortable beds and neat, so neat. We had forgotten how neat the world used to be.

And we have been here ninety-five days.

Sarah is running up the lawn yelling to me. She is holding a big silver fish from a hook and line. With a smile as wide as the river. Sarah is the smiling sister; she can't help it. She laughs and sings and gets so excited about things that do not seem worth all the excitement. That's what my other two sisters say. They don't say it nastily, just stating it matter-of-factly. They do love her too.

'You caught dinner, Sarah.'

'Look at this, brother, look at this, as silver as alfoil sheets, a mulloway from the depths of our river.'

'You are wonderful, elder sister by one.'

Sometimes at night while I am lying awake, I list out all the things that may happen, all the possible trajectories of our coming days. I stole the word trajectories from older sister by two, who likes four-syllable words. I think of the disappearances.

Think of Sarah and hope it won't be her. I also hope it will not be my other sisters.

In the house, we found a room full of old toys and board games. We play Monopoly in the late afternoon before it gets dark, as there is always the chance that the electricity will fail. Elder sister by three usually wins. She loves the names of the places on the board. I sometimes catch her, when she isn't looking, saying the names – Leicester Square, Park Lane, Mayfair, Oxford Street – silently as we play. She is much older and has been to London.

The house that we now call our own has a library. Mr Strattan was no doubt a scholarly man, said elder sister by three. A whole room with books in cases, from top to floor, on three walls, and a large window on the fourth wall overlooking the river. Elder sister by three cried when we first entered the room. She is one of those people, quaint folk says elder sister two, who still reads books. The ones made of paper where you turn the pages with your hands, and they do not need to be recharged. She often goes to the room and reads.

She says we have found Arcadia. A stately home in the country with books and views others would have once paid millions of dollars.

Sometimes we feel as though we are the only people left in the world. We have seen no other person in our ninety-five days at the Strattans' house. We don't talk about the time just before we arrived. It now seems too long ago to think about. When elder sister by three speaks of the ancient regime it is a story, a fable, a once-upon-a-time fairy tale. But we have remembered. Each day we run through set routines that we taught ourselves from before we arrived.

Elder sister by three loved the books that came with the house, but we all knew that there were more useful things that filled the rooms. The great sharp knives in the kitchen are one. They hung from walls or were kept in steel scabbards or waited innocently in drawers. We each have one of these knives strapped to our right legs. Sarah has made us our own scabbards so that we do not cut ourselves.

We never take them off.

We do not roam. At least one of us has to be within sight. We found whistles in the room with the toys and games; and wear them around our necks. We do not talk about these things now. They were organised in the first few days at the house. We imagine that we are on holidays in the country, but we know that the food will not last forever.

The future can arrive suddenly but we do not talk about it, though we must all be thinking of it, even eldest by one, Sarah, who seems to believe it is an extended holiday in a house of rich relatives.

It is the ninety-fourth day and we are making a fire in the fireplace to boil the water for our coffee and tea. We have plain biscuits with them. We have packs and packs of biscuits left in the cellar. The Strattans didn't indulge in chocolate or cream biscuits. There is an ease in the way we now make a fire and eat breakfast, as if there is nothing out there to kill us.

Having said that, none of us has seen a dead body. We just believe they are dead. In fact, they have simply disappeared. One day you would be talking to friends or neighbours and then you wouldn't see them again. It all seemed so sinister. No one to blame, no threats at the door, no one said anything.

The only thing we saw was a sign, a black spray of graffiti on a highway underpass that read, You need a knife, you must carry a knife. Written in huge script, twenty times or more on the wall.

It is the only advice we have had in all this time.

It does seem a long time ago, more than the ninety-five days. Some days they feel like somebody else's memories. None of my sisters speak of the time before we came to the house, so I rarely do and when I attempt to think about it, to form solid images and remember people and events, it blurs and I cannot be certain if it happened. Like an old person trying to remember yesterday. I try to think of my grandmother. I should have a grandmother, shouldn't I? But nothing.

So we live in the present. Talk about what we will do.

We finish breakfast and walk, all four of us arm in arm, down the grassed slope to the river below.

'Nobody can ever disappear us when we're arm in arm,' says Sarah, joy bursting from her. She sounds as if she has just discovered the formula to end all the evils of the world. 'No disappearing arm in arm, no disappearing arm in arm,' she chants.

Elder sister two and three are happy this morning. They smile at Sarah and agree. Together, as if rehearsed for a scene in a play, they say, 'Yes, sister, there will be no disappearing.'

We lay on the grass with our arms stretched. Four starfish beached. Eyes closed, feeling the warmth of a late spring morning. We are a thousand miles away from any danger. We are at the ends of the earth. Our touch our talisman.

The fish we eat from the river is our only meat. Sometimes we don't care if we eat meat or not. It is horrific to see the fish, bejewelled in silver armoury, die. To have to slip the knife, the one we have strapped to our leg, beneath its gills and slit off its head. We do not want to be reminded of death. Still, there are days when we hunger for meat and all four of us stand in the shallows with our lines in the water straining to catch a fish.

But today we are happy to lie on the grass. We do not look behind; are not wary of any danger; do not imagine sounds in the distance.

All four of us. There used to be five. I am sure. I sit up abruptly and my hands come free and the link is broken.

We had another sister.

'Sarah, we had another sister,' I look at my two other sisters: 'We had another sister'. I say it as if I am blaming them, as if they will deny it if I do not say it strongly.

But they don't. They nod sadly and agree. Chelsea, they say, Chelsea the fourth disappeared. Do not speak of it, brother.

So I don't but I know that I had almost forgotten her. I remembered it had been five, and it seemed so long ago that I had thought of her. As if she didn't exist, though it can only be months since she disappeared.

'Why am I the brother, sisters? Why can't we be four sisters?' The joy of the morning is gone and I want an answer.

'You have to be brother. You know why,' says elder sister by three.

'No, why do I?'

'You wear the pants and we wear dresses, that's why.'

'But I could wear a dress as easily as you.'

There is silence. Perhaps a sigh from two sisters.

'Then I will tell you, sister, who is also brother.'

There is a pause and I am waiting for her to speak, but she looks around the room, sees there is nowhere to go and continues. 'It is a small dispensation. They don't offer many.'

She looks at a cat that has suddenly appeared at the back-door. She hopes its presence is enough to halt what must be said, but her listeners do not notice.

'You are a boy so we could keep the family together. Women are sent elsewhere if there is not a male. One man to a household, no matter age or kinship.'

'What do you mean?'

'You would think that in a world that loses most its men to a virus that women would have a little more power, but they still run the show. The few that survived still hang onto power.'

'What do they want?'

'Just the same. Power. To assert themselves. Same old. We do it ourselves but men are naturally gifted in this area. We do not want to be breeders. We can keep together, keep the family together for as long as we can. Then we will see. We have the knives in case. They once in a place called Masada…never mind.'

'In case of what, sister?' And where is Masada?

'Just, in case. We will see. We will wait. We will meet them as a family.'

Outside the library

Outside the library, in an empty grassed block
there is a man casting a fishing line,
An older man with a hat, and if we looked closely,
may find a set of feathered lures. He casts
his line without effort, the nylon line
shimmering in its wavering arc.
Its movement through sky seems to spill water
as it makes a parabola. I imagine
he travels once a year to the far south
of New Zealand or Chile, away from
the warmth of this spare block, to fish for trout
in icy streams, that he in turn imagines
himself into a small figure amongst mountains,
as if the landscape were hieroglyphics,
as if the water could be caught and read.

Rain

She was annoyed that her female friends at the market were to get wiped from the earth by flood. They were good women who knew how to get a laugh out of life despite their layabout husbands. She was more annoyed with her husband and his almighty God, the same vengeful God who was planning to kill everyone on the earth, except her family. She didn't like his God. He was always demanding something. Do this, do that, just like her husband and her father before him.

Besides, what did his God ever do for him? The old boy was five hundred years old before they were able to conceive their first child. Then there were Shem, Ham and Japheth. It was his idea to call a son Ham.

Now he always had God talking to him, giving him instructions. Her life had been a list of instructions, prefaced by This is the Lord's Covenant, wife. She was sick of being called wife and his God seemed to only speak to men. It was always Go forth, Noah, or Take your sons, Shem, Ham and Japheth. The wives and daughters were tacked on the end, nameless.

While the boys were out cutting down gopher wood and collecting pairs of animals, she had slipped back into the town warning her friends that there might be a big storm coming. She didn't want to believe it and she was no doomsdayer like her husband, but she thought just in case she might make a few preparations.

Her husband would never admit it but she had an eye for carpentry. Knew how to get a straight angle and was better than him or his sons at getting a join to fit watertight. But Noah had kept the Ark to himself and his sons, telling her to keep to the kitchen. She would have hungry workers coming home every day. The monstrosity was half-finished in the backyard. Three hundred cubits in length, fifty in breadth and a height of thirty cubits. She could tell it would never float.

The last thing she was going to do was go aboard if the rains came. Not to mention the stench of all those filthy animals messing every day.

It was at this point that she decided that she would arrange the women from the basket-weaving group to get together a smaller boat. No grand title of Ark, but a well-made skiff with a good sail. They would take their cats.

When the clouds came in from the north, she had a premonition that this was going to be a big storm, the one that hit once every century. They had happened before and people had survived and gone on living.

It was when the lightning struck that she had gathered up the women and they had gone to the boat, climbing aboard with a few supplies and their cats, Zillah bringing a nice eggplant casserole for the first night.

Sitting around the table, they felt the bottom rise. The boat was afloat and they could feel its slow rock that gradually settled down to a steady rhythm. Their smiles breaking open like parting waters.

She had said, 'Wives,' waiting for a moment of suspense, 'no longer. We shall now choose a name. A name that will be our own.'

They had thought briefly, each woman announcing it as they went around, one by one, around the table.

It was only when they got to the last two women that they realised these two with large shawls and scarves over their heads were not women at all. Asked to take off their disguises, they found two young men, handsome boys who had just come into town. It seemed that Zillah had brought more than her moussaka.

And all the women saw what was brought aboard, and behold, it was very good.

On the Roof

The three sons are on the roof mending the ridge caps, mortaring the cracks, cleaning the gutters. It is a mother's day gift. They would like to say it is an act of love long overdue, but they want her to sell.

I have never really noticed the garden till I am on the roof. My mother has a bird bath, a little bird house for them to rest. It hangs from a hook in the tree like a square uterus, its dark whale eye staring around the yard. She tells me the doves live in the sheoak; she comes out at dawn and feeds them. There are magpies that walk up the backsteps, crows whose whoosh of wings she hears from the kitchen, the occasional kookaburra and lorikeet. Where would she go if she couldn't feed the birds?

On the roof, I stare into the jacaranda and see her life of busying herself: years cooking pots of soup or roast dinners, even the shank broths made for her dogs, are no longer needed. It must be lonely at night, till she hears the birds crazy with morning.

We all agree she is getting worse with age, she is half-mad and stubborn. She had been good with small children and animals, things that were helpless and loyal, but now all the grandchildren have grown up, her dogs died years ago and are buried side by side in the backyard. There is nothing left but these stupid birds.

From the roof, I look across the hibiscus, the morning glory engulfing the fence. I hear the birds in the old jarrah tree, the doves are speckled along the ground, my mother must have just fed them.

Perhaps the roof will hold, I tell my brothers, as I fill in the cracks, rip out the loose concrete and tuck the mortar, using my fingers for the first time, at last ready to dirty my hands.

late night swimming

we light a fire on the beach and walk
into dark water, thanking the gods,
little and small, for the full moon above.
it hovers over us, maternal & expectant,
perhaps wanting prayers from us this warm night,
offering its light in exchange for something
we never knew we had lost. swimming out to
the moon, our heads constantly turning,
fixing the fire to know our way back.

At our Grandmother's

Our teacher gave us the task of writing a poem entitled 'At our Grandmother's'. He read out an example and told us to create a distinctive voice. It is always the voice that will make it convincing, he told us – at least twice a day. He means well. The house in the poem sounded a bit creepy as did granny for that matter. Posh, though. Lots of references to jewellery, expensive furniture and death.

The problem is I have one surviving grandmother who only drops in two or three times a year. The visit starts out nice and friendly. Granny pulls up in a taxi and treads delicately down the front path with a box of cakes from David Jones, but by late afternoon there's a fight brewing. When Gran gets angry at my mum, she usually pulls out a small silver flask of whisky and lights a cigarette. Two things my Mum does not approve of in her house. The ritual of grandma's exile is then reenacted again, though Mum calls it the *Prodigal Mother Who Doesn't Get a Second Chance.*

I don't even know where my grandmother lives. No one in the family has ever been to her abode so it's difficult to write a poem. My mum tells me to make it up. Use your imagination, that's what you should be doing in poetry. Teachers have no right getting students to write personal things about family. I try to explain that our teacher wants it to be authentic. I say this word in a fancy way knowing it will annoy my mum. She phffs like a horse, looks me in the eye to see if I am trying to pull a swifty on her and then says in an exaggerated slangy voice, Just make it rhyme, love.

Mum would have made a good actor, my father often says. That mother of yours can be five women in one day. I'm always hoping one of them will be half decent, he jokes.

Mum doesn't smile.

I mention my dilemma to my friend, Laurie, but he fails to show satisfactory sympathy. 'What's your problem? Both my grannies are dead. I'm thinking about writing about the cemetery. My sister says Gothic is in.'

I only ever understand half the things Laurie says. As for his sister, she is really out there in a strange good-looking sort-of-way. My mum says she's got it coming. 'What, Mum, got what?' 'Do your homework, Robbie.' 'But Mummy, my name's not Robbie.' It's a little joke we have.

I try and find out how the rest of the guys are going with their poems and they all seem surprisingly pleased with the assignment. They tell me about their grandparents and how they love them more than their Mum and Dad. They give more expensive presents, things their parents refuse to buy them.

Presents? No one told me about this. The odd sponge cake randomly delivered by an unpredictable ancestor hardly counts.

I scout around and find out about this complex web of relationships between these boys and grandparents. Not one other granny turns up in a taxi with a flask or is thrown out of the house. They are seen regularly, and their place of abode is known and visited, sometimes staying overnight. There is suddenly a totally new world out there I was unaware of, that existed like a parallel universe. *Sliders* or *Dr Who* style. I seem to be the only one excluded. Laurie doesn't count because of his sister.

I take this information home with a purpose. 'Why have I been deprived of a rich and psychologically rewarding relationship with my grandmother?' I ask.

My mum almost laughs, an act she rarely commits. 'My son, the stand-up. At least you're funnier than your father. That woman you wish to have a rich, psychological relationship with, is incapable, at a cognitive and empathetic level, of your desired wish. Most cultures have myths and folklore that explain women like my mother. In Norway they are called the huldra. Look it up, kid. Maybe you could write a poem about that.'

And that was as far as I got. Still, I knew I was missing out on a significant part of my childhood development and definitely missing the story that would explain my mother's relationship with her mother, and explain a lot about Mum. I also start to worry about all the other things that I have failed to notice. I have seen Dennis with his grandparents and he did mention to me how they went on holiday together. Mick has his grandmother living with them. Why have I never registered these families that were different to my own? It was like they were invisible to me.

When dinner is finished, I stay seated with my mother. She is reading the newspaper so I sit quietly and stare at her.

She doesn't look up but says slowly, 'What are you looking at?'

'My mother,' I say chirpily.

Then she looks up. 'And what have you noticed, my dear son?'

I think quickly. 'Your hair. I always thought it was black, but it's not quite dark enough for black. Is there a name for that colour?

'This is starting to get weird, Rob. Is this about the poem? You're not using me as your grandmother, are you?'

'No, you're much too young and attractive.'

'Now you are worrying me.'

I think I have her where I want her now. 'I was getting worried about the things I don't notice. I've been at it for a day and there is already a long list.'

'Such as?'

'Given time, it might be everything. Well firstly, we're always told we are all equal and that we should be kind and thoughtful to others. Everyone agrees on this: school, you, Dad, the United Nations. But I noticed there are many exceptions.'

'Be specific.'

'Well, I can just tell that our teacher doesn't like the new boy from East Pakistan and half the class are nasty and bully him, even though he hasn't done anything wrong.'

'So, have you done anything to rectify this state of affairs?'

'No, I told you I just noticed since I've started to think about it. I might have been unpleasant to him as well. Everyone else is.'

'Your point?'

'That's it. There's a whole world that's going unnoticed. I'm living in this world but only seeing a tiny angle of it.'

'This is quite profound for a twelve-year-old. Maybe it's the poetry.'

'On one side of our fence we have Mrs Cann, who you don't like because she's a snob and walks around like she can only breathe "rarefied air", your words, and then Mrs Lamone on the other side, who you say is not the right sort. The only reason being that she drinks too much coffee, smokes too much and is a divorcee.'

All is quiet. I may have gone too far. Perhaps I should have slowly worked my way up to my mother's flaws.

She has turned away and is looking out the window. I am looking around to see if there is a clear passage if I need to make a dash.

Finally, she says, 'And your father?'

'Dad?' I almost shout out.

'Yes, any astute observations on your father?'

I breathe again. 'Well, you know how you like watching ballet and Dad gets really uncomfortable. He has a name for the guys in the tights. I think it's just because they're wearing tight pants.'

She looks at me and says, 'You might be right. About the tight pants, that is.' She folds the newspaper, pulls back her chair and walks out.

I did have some other things to tell her: why are cars built to do over a hundred mph when the limit is sixty-five mph and most driving needs to be done at less than forty mph? The way America invades another country, Vietnam at present, killing thousands and then present themselves convincingly as 'good'? It is 1970 after all! Also, whatever happened to my grandfather. I have never thought about it.

Anyway, I still have a poem to write in less than three days. An authentic poem that I have to invent without a grandmother.

I went to the library and found a poem by Hart Crane and it's about his grandmother's letters. That's a good idea. I could get little-known gran writing letters to my non-existent grandfather. Hart also calls rain 'soft', which I like.

After dinner, my mother tells me to stay at the table. I am

about to ask about Grandpa – sounds strange saying it for the first time – but she interjects, 'My turn.'

'Your grandmother was my birth mother but that's all. She left me very early and I was brought up in foster homes. She turned up after I was married. Standing at the flywire door after twenty-five years, wanting to come in. She's allowed visits but that's all.'

'What about my grandfather?'

'Took you a while to ask about him. One of the invisibles, hey? Well, there is no grandfather. Unknown, unseen and unwanted. Anything else?'

I nod and she gets up to leave but I ask if she has any letters written by Gran.

'No, just a postcard,' she says. 'It was sent from Aden in the early days. Despite all I've said about her, she was an adventurous woman. Great shot of the camels. I'll get it for you but I want it back – for the camel, not my mother.'

I finished up inventing a scene where she is writing home to her daughter from a tent she was living in, outside of Aden. It was not exactly 'at my grandmother's' but I wrote a short note telling my teacher that my grandmother was a bohemian who travelled the world and had many abodes. He wrote a note back telling me not to use 'abode' so often. Nevertheless, he was impressed with my poem, probably because after constantly reminding us to be specific I described her 'living quarters' as a 'black goat-hair tent' and gave the Arabic name of bayt al-shar. I got 88%.

Three months later, a policeman came to the door and asked for Mum. Her mother had been found dead in her house. She was asked to go with him.

We all went there a few days later to pick up her personal items. There wasn't much and as I looked around her home thought that I would have liked to have asked my grandmother about the desert, camels and Aden.

I knew I would have written a better poem had I seen the one room flat, with one plate, a cup and saucer, one pot and a small heater.

The Clocks

I won't have a clock in the house now,
prefer to wait in the night not knowing
if there are minutes or hours before sunrise.

I sometimes hear the luxury car next door start
in the dark, like a great cat ready to hunt,
and know it is almost time.

In summer there are raucous birds
but winter keeps it darkness close
and I won't keep a clock

reminding me of the small leavings
and great grievings that time
drags behind in deep freeze.

The healing of time they like to say,
the incessant grounding and pounding
of the heel on your throat they keep quiet.

There are no wars, no declarations,
not even rocks thrown, just walls slowly
appearing, leaving a space fitting an anchorite.

The old australia

My mother spoke of it admiringly.
My father its silent embodiment: masculine, reticent, irreverent.
Came home at the end of the day covered in dirt & sweat;
a joke to downplay despair, and a philosophy of
expecting things to finish arse-about.
As kids we had the sun and beach to act out our identities.
It browned and toughened our skins,
made our eyes sensitive to light,
made us arrogant with health, suspicious
of those who couldn't swim or run.
My uncle looked a bit like Errol Flynn, liked women and beer.
Could load three tons of concrete onto a truck himself,
worked from dawn to dust,then smoked a few rollies,
drank a couple of king browns in the truck homebound.
My mother called these men *real* men,
then spoke with yearning for Richard Tauber, Vienna & opera,
wondering why she was screwed up.
Tauber, the *other* man, was a secret my father would never know.
We were free & isolated, safe & classless,
sympathised with a straight blonde stare with
the downtrodden who couldn't set their own lands straight,
but still thought them stupid bastards. We gave the finger,
thought ourselves larrikins, never thinking of revolution,
which belonged to foreign types.

G

He woke to what might have been an animal sound and sensed she was outside the window. He jumped out of bed and leaned into the darkness, seeing her staring up at him, not saying a word. 'I'll be three minutes, I'll grab some apples.'

They walked down the hill and saw the back reefs breaking like white flowers against a darkness that was just shifting beyond that moment where the edge between night and day tips to a soft shadowless visibility. Then walked along the coast road to the Point, their boards beneath their arms appearing in the darkness as either weapons or celestial wings.

They had been going down the beach together every day during the holidays since they met. He was hand-fishing on the reef when he noticed a girl coming down the sandhill. He turned back, concentrating on the tension of the line, lifting it slightly so it went taut, so any nibble would be noticed. Then she was there, only two steps away from him, already preoccupied with her bait being fixed securely, and focusing solely on the water below her.

They didn't speak and even when she caught a fish and Roald congratulated her, she ignored him. When leaving, he said goodbye and began walking up the sandhill. Near the top, he realised she was behind him, walking slowly now, though she must have run up the hill to have been so close. They crossed the coast road side by side and walked up his street, until at his house he turned and told her he was going in for lunch.

She spoke for the first time. It didn't sound like a fourteen-year-old's voice. More like a voice that had been fermented for years in a barrel or maybe a well, sounding as if it came from a distant place.

'You live 'ere?'

'We moved in last week.'

'What you doin'?'

'Just having lunch.'

'You comin' out after?'

'I suppose.'

'I'll come back and wait outside for you.'

That had been six weeks ago and they had been inseparable, though she didn't talk very often and he knew almost nothing about her. She came to meet him every day. When the surf was on the rise, she would go to his back window before dawn so they could get to the Point before the crowd. Other days, she would sit and wait on the front verge and they would go to the beach and bodysurf or fish or roam the bush north of where the road ended.

There had been only three days when they had not spent their days together. G stayed with her uncle on occasions; she didn't say why but said it was always for three days. He would pick her up and take her home with him. It was just at the end of these three days, during the middle of the night, that Roald heard a skateboard, the clunking roll of tiny hard wheels on asphalt, and knew it was G. His room didn't face the road but he stuck his head out the window to try to hear her. The moon was almost full and he could see it tangled in their jacaranda in the backyard.

Next morning, G was sitting on the verge. She had a skateboard and he could see she was proud of her new acquisition.

She held it up as if she were presenting it formally to him. 'Look. My uncle gave it to me.'

Roald liked the idea that G was an anonymous being who had suddenly appeared like a mythical sprite without parents, a proper name or home, though he knew she lived only a half-mile away, but the skateboard and the existence of an uncle made G, the girl with an initial as a name, connected to a more prosaic world.

The skateboard was not new and was a little battered, but he said it was great. 'I heard you go down the hill last night.'

'Did you? I wanted you to. It was almost a full moon.' It came out fast and staccato.

She did something then that she had never done. She raised her chin and pretended to be a wolf and made a low howling sound that made Roald think of dark forests in fairytales, but then it shifted to what sounded like the purring of a great cat. She had never been not her, never acted or spoke without being prompted. She was always G: quiet, unanimated, never joking, without irony or artifice. Now she seemed play-acting.

'Do your parents let you out in the middle of the night?'

'They're dead asleep.'

The first thing Roald's mum said when she saw G was that she looked like a street urchin. That hair of hers, and what was she wearing.

G was tall for her age, skinny, suntanned and had sun-bleached straw for hair. Roald had not noticed at first but her clothes did look worn-out. They were faded as if all the colour had been washed away.

On their way home from the Point, they would stop at the shop overlooking the bay. G would roll cigarettes – she carried an old packet of Drum, the plastic cover almost worn away, which she refilled each week by stealing from her mum's pack – and Roald would buy a carton of milk and choc milk and they'd sit at the stool table and look out to Rottnest. Then they would walk home on the path that ran along the ocean, saying little and always an arm's distance between them. He didn't know what that space meant but it was there: along the coast road, on the beach, through bush tracks, it was there.

One day looking out at Rottnest after a day at the Point, G started speaking. 'We went to Rottnest. Me and my mum and dad and my brother. I was coming down a big hill with my brother on the front of the bike. I pedalled as hard as I could, then I put my feet on the handlebar.' She drew back on her cigarette.

Roald heard the inhalation of breath, the small sigh.

'We come off. I scrapped all the back of my legs and bum. My brother hit his head on the road. It was sharp bitch'men. The blood was all over it.'

G had never spoken so many words at one time. She was staring out at Rottnest, the island a mirage of grey castles and cliffs. Roald didn't know if he should say anything, then asked how long ago the accident was.

'I was ten and my brother was eight.'

When it came out, the event turned into words, it seemed to Roald that G appeared surprised, as though she had never said it before and now spoken was different to the thing she remembered in her head – that block of wood, the black sludge – that she had been carrying for nearly four years. She shrugged and went back to looking out at the ocean, then lit another rollie and gave it to him.

A moment later, she said she couldn't have a bike now, and then in another voice, not her own, she muttered lowly, 'That will teach you for killing my son.'

'What did you say?'

'Nothin'.'

He was thinking about G's brother when his mum came into the kitchen and hugged him.

'Have you been smoking? Has that girl given you cigarettes?' She was a woman who didn't wait to hear answers she already knew. 'I heard from Marguerite who just lives over the hill, and a few houses up from your girlfriend.'

'She's not my girlfriend,' Roald interjected, hoping to turn the subject away from him smoking.

'Well, your friend then, the one you spend every day with from dawn to dusk. She said that the family is a wreck. Her mother spends most of her day in bed on tranquillisers. Drinking coffee and smoking cigarettes.' She stopped and looked her son in the eyes. 'And the father is a real no-hoper. Never worked a hard day in his life, has tattoos all the way up his arms, and heaven knows where else, and is a heavy drinker.'

She also wanted to mention how the girl roamed the street at night and that there was no one at home to control her, no school in her life, and just too much freedom for a girl her age. Marguerite told her G had a 'history'. But she decided that was for another time.

Towards the end of the holidays, Roald and G stopped at Mick's, his best friend who had been in Ireland with his family. Roald threw his board on the lawn and went to the front door while G walked up the long gradient of street with her skateboard.

Mick came out from the beneath the house where he had

been playing table tennis and called to Roald. Mick was telling him how he had missed out on summer and Ireland was fucking freezing, before his older brother appeared.

Greg never uttered a sentence without its sole purpose being an insult or a laugh. He was usually laughing as he said it, and only stayed for as long as it took to deliver his lines. He laughed out the line, 'Priests and nuns everywhere. Mum and Dad had a fucking ball. Thought it the last stop before heaven.'

Just then, G came down the street on her skateboard.

Greg watched her flick her skateboard into her hand and said, 'Well, who's this, then?'

'She's a friend,' Roald said too loudly.

'Roald found himself a girlfriend over the holiday, while the competition was out of town.'

'Get lost.'

'Mind that language, young man,' Greg laughed out. 'Must be a real summer romance if you get so heat up…' He stopped and looked at G. 'Hey, is that the girl who gave Mark…'

Before he had the word out, Roald ran straight at him and gave him a hip and shoulder to the chest. He had no inkling that he would ever do that off the football field but for a second he was standing there with the older boy flat on his back having trouble breathing.

As Roald and G walked away, he heard Greg spluttering, 'You little mad shit. Fuck you and take your mole.'

They didn't say anything till they were nearly home and Roald asked why she never talked about her parents. She didn't reply but sort of shrugged.

Roald tried again. 'If you had to use one word to describe your mum, what would it be?

'Sad.'

'And your dad?'

'He's a cunt.'

She wasn't on the verge the next day. When she didn't turn up the following day, Roald walked over the hill and went to her house. It wasn't quite as bad as he expected, so he walked up the stairs and knocked.

The woman who appeared looked young but as Roald observed her, she seemed to grow older.

'Excuse me, I'm a friend of G. I was wondering if she was home.'

G's mother was wearing an old cardigan though it was a hot morning.

'I'm sorry,' she said, and Roald really thought she meant it. 'She's staying with her uncle.'

'When will she return, if you don't mind me asking?'

'I don't know.' Pausing before she continued, 'I don't know,' and walked away without closing the door.

When Roald returned three days later, there was no one home and it felt like a house abandoned. It was almost the end of the holidays, though there was a good month of summer left.

The following day, there was an unseasonal storm, the remnants of a dying cyclone that had trekked south but had turned out to sea and had lost strength.

The Fifties

holden caulfield's a young pinko
who should have stayed at school
if mccarthy had his way which he does most days
looking all hawk-like even in his double-breaster
talonned with good old fashioned values
that could disembowel lefties & deviants
(had a theory sodom & gomorrah were early
communist factions & lot's wife a cadre)
he's god-proud to be an american
god's country where you can buy
wringer-washers in red and blue stripes
drive a cadillac down avenues as wide as a wildwesttown
and everybody watches lucy

elsewhere everyone is fucking tired of imperialists:
castro & che climb down from the sierra maestra in their beards
and enter havana smoking big cigars
viet cong climb out of holes in the ground
perch in trees & the militarists don't like
the way war is not being played properly
beatniks are beating bongos
and ginsberg howls into an acetylene sky
about all the best minds of a generation
someone has invented teenagers
and they dance into the streets gyrating thighs & leather
and holden probably wishes he's dean or brando

it's an existentialist smirk they might
have stolen off camus
or those other heathens in dying europe
who know that fresh faces widen in isolation
and fought tanks with their bare hands in budapest

but they know how to create reality in the land of the me:
they know there's more than one way to skin a prat
and though star wars is twenty years away
it is just the script they want
and if a-bombs & h-bombs won't do it
then coke, pepsi & mcdonalds will
and everybody watches lucy

and there is space as if we needed another metaphor
pointy bits that penetrate the sky heading towards a longing moon
though the ruskies get their first
sending up a dog called laika who circles till he runs out of bark
but everyone loves a dog story & an adventure to the moon
boys grow up wanting to be astronauts instead of train drivers
and it's pity about the third world
but we know we've never had it so good
as a prime minister will one day tell us.

Almost

They stared out on a late afternoon sea, not a breath of wind, not a cloud.

'Almost the end of summer,' he said.

'Few good days left.' She turned her head away from him, looked up the coast as if autumn might just arrive around the corner, then added, 'April…always some fine, warm days. Less wind.'

He sat on the sand, the tiny waves sometimes reaching his feet, his knees up and his arms resting on them. She kept her arms by her sides.

After a minute, he said, 'That ship that's been in Gage Roads all summer – it's finally leaving, going north by the look of it.'

They sat in silence for another minute or two. It was not uncomfortable; they enjoyed the soft heat of late afternoon, the still blue water.

'I think you would die without the ocean.' After a moment's hesitation, she went on, 'You're like one of those amphibians – come on land for a while but always have to return or they dry up. You would go all scaly and dehydrate. Just stop breathing.'

In the distance, a mirage of cloud pretended it was a high looming cliff. A large, craggy island of Norse legend, though it was only flat, sandy Rottnest.

'If you had to say the one thing you loved about me, what would it be?'

He didn't pause, didn't wonder how it might sound. 'There is nothing superfluous about you.'

'That's OK, I quite like that.'

He turned his head slightly towards her. 'So?'

'Yes.'

'When?'

'Tomorrow.'

'Did you know that we only ever saw each other during the day. Not once after sunset.'

'I know. It would have never lasted.' She nodded. 'It wasn't real in a way. As if we stole something and thought that since no one caught us, we could put it back the way we found it, as if nothing had changed.'

'Lot of ifs in that sentence.'

There is a small space, only a few centimetres, between them but they never touch.

'So, tomorrow then,' he said. 'Who will I swim with? I will be twenty-three tomorrow and you will be flying home to New Haven with your parents to marry the man on the yacht.'

She waited for the last comment to dissipate, allowed it to lose its weight. 'See, it was a summer romance.'

He nodded, 'Yes, you were right, of course. A summer romance. We really did carry on over nothing.'

'You went crazy there for a while. So did I. We're better now.'

'Absolutely. Sane as…'

'As?'

'Nothing comes to mind. I'm having trouble thinking of things that are sane.'

'You will. You always have words for everything.'

They looked back out to sea. A sea tern had just dived from a great height and had re-emerged with a silver flash of fish that it was now wrestling with. Probably wondering whether to swallow and take the chance of choking or just letting it go.

Photographs

Here you are, eighteen or nineteen, looking
out of the frame as if you could never die.
In denim and black boots, hair to the shoulders
looking like David Cassidy, though you
may have preferred someone more hardcore.
Here we are, an old timber mill with a winch
around our necks like a shark hook. All of us.
Us five. In the next, fishing at dusk, looking
wild & elemental on a deserted beach.
You're still sending photos, sitting up in a hospital
bed, tubes in your nose, managing to laugh.
Some days the morphine made you hallucinate:
the hospital room alive with birds in flight,
cats in their lithe limbs as graceful as sleep.
At home a few days later you ask me
to select a photo for the funeral service,
talking as if you were going to photograph
it yourself. You had six albums on the table,
old fashioned, thick tombs of photos of us
in out late teens: surfing Cobblestones,
on the side of the road outside Sandfire,
hitching in the red dirt. Leaning on your
Charger at the shearing sheds. The Iron Clad
in Marble Bar where we had been half-kidnapped
by a half-mad miner who wanted a drink.
These things we did as if we had been
wild kites not attached to the earth,
needing only wind to breathe.

Cuttlefish

We were born by the ocean, knew its shifting
> face by wind and moon. Tracks through dunes, the yellow
>> flowers of sour fig in season, bluebottles

washed ashore like plastic toys, the white chalk
> holsters of cuttlefish. A perfect day
>> was hot, still, with a heaving swell. We were

transgressive in summer, heroic and brash.
> The blue sky allowed us to conceive
>> of anti-gods, thinking our parents' gods

too pale, too quiet. Never reckless enough
> for our liking. We knew the shifting wind,
>> fickle moon. We learnt the warm seasons,

and they were too brief. When winter came,
> we were halves of self, strewn along the beach
>> like cuttlefish, whose beauty only seen beneath water.

Melancholia

(from Albrecht Dürer's *Melancholia 1*)

She once stood on a beach, sand beneath her, Sea of Galilee ahead, sky above, and understood.

She has not used her wings for years and though her feet grip the earth with an intimacy that surprises her, she misses flight. Her friends tell her it's all in her head, there are now people who can help, professionals not shamans. I am sad not mad, she says. They are not unrelated, they tell her, and bring her buttercup and watercress to put in her hair. It will help, they say, but she feels the weight on her head, like the keys hanging from her dress. So many competing explanations. There is the sphere in front of her, its perfection mocking the granite octo-hedron, with its sharp lines, pointed and aggressive. Her dear greyhound also suffers, stuck between the two. Its ribs show through like broken half-circles.

Always behind me that damn square of numbers, another conundrum suggesting an order that must be, if only we had the right questions. They tell me my complexion darkens be-cause of the black bile that rises. I am as white as an angel, I joke, white as hallucination, chant friends who now appear like a Greek chorus, painted and masked. The death bell hangs above the square, the hourglass to its side. There is a connection they wish me to see, so I stare ahead, compass in hand, con-structing arcs, measuring sides, testing the ratios with sequences of number in the square. All numbers – vertical, horizontal, diagonal – adding to thirty-four. I look around for my tools – straight edge, hammer, saw and nails. I shall build a house, a temple, a lighthouse. Such purpose would solve my melancholia, allow me to rise again into the firmament. Meanwhile, I stay unsolved, open to glances, to the speculations of observers.

Some see me as the Artist-figure waiting inspiration: the moody, brooding melancholic who seeks the word to release beauty. In the room of mathematical objects, tools of creation, oppressive time darkens my skin, though the sea, the far shore with its colours, its promised light, wait to be written. I have walked upon that shore, I was never really an angel, the wings a deception, my flights inwards. I have brought home shells, memorised the artistry of weed strewn on its edges. I taught myself to observe, to say less. Hoping to find a method.

Beware the word: it is not as it seems. I may have wings and am no angel but can tell you there is no Devil. Or any lesser demons who may have possessed me. Words they invent to define. Later they will use the word melancholy kindly, necessary in the disposition of a poet. I am ancient and have seen the meanings shift and slide over time. I spent a night with Mary Magdalene, another cursed with devils, along the shores of that harp-shaped Sea of Galilee. We talked and ate and drank wine. Mary and I agreed we were sometimes glad to be alive. Still, it appears again, the dark brooding, the array of choices which are meant to save me.

I was here well before the artist.

1514 – the year it is drawn, appearing inside his magical square, the year Copernicus asserts the earth moves, while the sun stands still. The year Titian paints *Noli me Tangere*. It is all here in this room, the fear it instils, the loss of certainty that geometry brings – proofs and predictions, angles and angels, a future where numbers and signs offer greater truths.

They are right and they are wrong. A kite, a song.

Two different things all together.

There are other days when I accept the drawing is about his mother's death. Grief and loss.

Youth is the Thing that Leaps & Jumps

There has never been a God, just smaller
deities, mildly wild and indifferent,
spinning lines & coins, that you mistook for luck.
They spoke in riddles & codes, and believing
you could outwit them, you grew careless, the slow
wearing went unnoticed, things that crept, crept.
The wild deities you wagered on were never
to blame. Parents growing too old, becoming
other people, a friend's spine pasted
together after a rare cancer, now four
inches shorter, a loved cat dying.
You rarely used the word grief till it appeared,
casual & swaggering at the open door,
reminding you of someone you once knew.

A Pinch of Salt

She knew it would be one of those days. She had burnt the eggs for breakfast, the goat had pissed in the house and now, before she had time for an afternoon nap, there were two angels at her door.

Good-looking boys, both of them. Tall and blond, a trait unknown around these parts, and they had a way of mysteriously moving around the house, which she wasn't sure about. Nevertheless, there they were, all serious now, talking to her husband, and from what she could overhear, they wanted the family to just pack up and leave.

Unfortunately, their high cheekbones and unblemished skin had not gone unnoticed in the twin cities, known for their debauchery. Soon there were the local louts bashing at the door, demanding her husband to release the two boys. 'Come on, you old sod, keep 'em for yourself, will ya.'

She knew her husband was a good man, as he often told her, but she believed she had tired of his goodness. Her day so far had only made it worse. It might have been a small thing but when he introduced her to the angels as the Wife, it occurred to her that she hadn't heard her name spoken aloud for years, and feared that she might forget it herself.

Being a good man, a man of propriety and duty, he had gone to the door himself, defiant and with a characteristic paternal attitude that occasionally annoyed others. She had been proud of her husband as he had stood up to the raging mob outside, telling them that the two men were his guests; they knew the duty of the host to protect his guests.

She had softened for a moment, thinking, yes, he did have his good points, when she heard her husband tell the raging mob, still in his stentorian voice, that they could not have these men, these men of God, but could have his two daughters, still virgins.

She felt the blood run to her face and in that second of recognition knew that he had gone too far this time. Years of him rambling on Yahweh this, Yahweh that, the silly little rituals that he made her go through. Besides, he was too old for her. He was an old sod like they said. She still had some good years left in her.

She had rushed forward to stop this old man from giving away her daughters, but had been grabbed by one of the angels, while the other angel slammed shut the door. This same angel had now turned and told the family to get out the back door and go into the mountains before God destroyed the twin cities with fire. She should have known all along that God would be involved. Given no time to protest, she was ushered out the door, through the city gates and into the wilderness.

She had been wondering what her first step would be, where she could go now and how she could slip away. It was not long after that she heard an almighty explosion, a flash of light that lit the sky and felt the heat on the back of her head. Since they had left the city gates, her husband had been yabbering something about turning around, but she had not listened.

She had turned round with the intention of asking the old gasbag what he had said, but didn't have time to get the words out.

Rats

I took the axe from the back shed
and stood over the rat on the lawn.
We had tried killing the rats with poison,
complained about the noise in the roof
and now the cat had brought him to me:
Traumatised, claws fixed into the grass,
eyes staring out. No more than a large mouse,
someone's pet. I waited axe in hand
for longer than was manly. My father
would have ended it by now. As kids
kittens had disappeared with a knock on
the head, even our dog who swallowed plastic.
We had tried killing the rats with poison
but killing is hard face to face.
I went inside hoping it would go away,
thinking how language invents words that make
it right to kill: pests, vermin, infestations.
How it was no longer right to kill a whale.
Endangered, whale-song. It is hard to love a rat.
Hard to kill a rat. I carry him out
to the back lane in a pool net,
finding him a place in the high grass
where the crows might not get him.

Faustus Hood

He was only five months into the marriage when he realised this was not how he imagined it. Something had changed in those one hundred and fifty days. His wife was slowly transforming. Just the other morning, he had looked across the pillow and her nose with a tiny bump near the bridge was straight, the three freckles on her cheek darker.

There were many things the same. They still had sex, still talked, liked being home together. But Gregory felt an encroaching tide would soon draw back and expose some other Cicely.

He loved her eyes; almond eyes whose lids darkened on the corners like the paintings of women favoured by Renaissance artists. He remembered the first time they met. She was standing on the edge of water staring at him as he came out of the ocean, finally saying, You belong in the sea.

He noticed her eyes.

She had always looked into his eyes. He thought it was a game and had stared back, thinking he had to outstare her. But she never looked into his eyes now. It was like she was looking just to the left as if he had a parrot on his shoulder.

Perhaps they needed children. They were successful enough to have an architecturally designed home in a beach suburb. If there were children, they could go to the beach, go on picnics, and the children would go to elite private schools and meet other elite children.

Gregory woke one morning and heard Cicely making breakfast and thought, so it will be like this, and was not deeply disappointed. When she came to say it was time, he couldn't recognise the woman at the door, and she stared slightly to the left, refusing to admit that he also was unrecognisable.

Grave(s)

Aleksandar had lived alone in his house since 1995. Eleven years of living alone; eleven years since the war ended. No one in that time had ever arrived in the middle in the night, but when he heard the knock, Aleksandar got up out of his bed as if it was expected. Lit a cigarette, turned on the front light and opened the door.

The man at the door was dishevelled, looking as if he had been on the road for a week. He spoke first, in a voice that was used to being obeyed. 'Turn off that light,' then walked inside. 'Do you know me?'

Aleksandar looked at him. It was like seeing a before-and-after photograph of a middle-aged and much older man. He knew this man. Beneath the deep furrows, watery eyes and thinning grey hair there was a man he once knew.

'I know you, cousin.'

'Good. I will live here with you then.'

'Yes, cousin.'

That was the first night of the five years that the two men would live together. In the morning, they drank coffee and ate eggs. They talked little. Aleksandar didn't know what things he could say.

'I thought you were living in the capital.'

When the man spoke, he would nod slowly and jut out his jaw slightly. 'I did until it became too unsafe. They changed the laws, kowtowing to the enemy. It was no longer safe.'

There was no uneasiness between them and the conversations were short. Aleksandar had a small house with a few chickens, pigs and sheep. He had once lived in the capital, working in a factory. He had been to war. Then it was no longer the city he once knew. He went north to the country and had tried to survive by selling whatever he could produce on the farm.

There was a shack across the farmyard where the man slept. Aleksandar worked in the fields, went into the village, and never asked the man what he did each day.

A week after he arrived, the man told Aleksandar that he had some money. He would put in for expenses. 'Money and two guns is all I have,' he said.

It took months before the subject of the war was broached.

The man said to his cousin, 'You know I did everything for our country, for our people.'

Aleksandar had replied honestly, 'I do. We all do. It is a crime what has happened.'

'It is, cousin. It is. I know I will be caught soon. Someone will tell someone else and there is the reward. I know people are capable of anything.'

Some days, Aleksandar would come home and find a freshly made cake on the table beneath a cloth, the man having found enough eggs around the yard. Aleksandar would have liked to have eaten one piece with a coffee and make it last the week, but his cousin preferred to eat it all at once and go without for a week.

One night, they had a special dinner. It was Aleksandar's sixtieth birthday and they drank slivovitz into the night.

The man seemed to lose some of the tenseness that held him together. 'Do you remember my father? No, you wouldn't.

He fought alongside Tito's partisans during the war. A brave man killed by Croatians who had allied themselves with Hitler. Sixty years ago, the year I was born. He was buried somewhere in the mountains, but I didn't know where. I went looking for his grave. I even had troops looking for it. Nothing came of it till I spoke to a Muslim man on a small trail in the mountains of Bosnia-Herzegovina. He showed me where it might be found, and there it was, hardly hidden at all, my father's grave in a small valley. It was a beautiful place, a good place for a grave. I was so grateful that when the war began I spared that man's village. Bradina. Just a small Muslim village, but I ordered the men to leave it as it was. I pay my debts.'

He never spoke about his life after that night. Conversations were about the weather, the health of the animals, the search for chicken's eggs around the yard.

No one was sure if there had been an informer. The police arrived. Twenty of them from the Special Unit, wearing black and masked, with orders of bringing the man in alive so he could be tried for genocide at the World Court in The Hague. They were younger men in their twenties, specially selected for their youth, so they had no old allegiances.

They had expected to come face to face with a monster, a mass murderer, the general who had ordered the slaughter of thousands; the man responsible for a great hole in the forest where they buried Muslim men and young boys. Instead, there was an old man walking slowly around the front garden. When they burst through the gate swaggering artillery that could have destroyed a small town, he had stood still, looking at them with a smile stretched across his face like barbed wire.

South of Eve

He had come home
after nights of amnesia
in bottles of bourbon
the familiar lamplit limbs
he had melted into.

Coming home to Caitlin
believing that her mouth
like a massacre
dark & bloody
could heal him
take him off this wrong trail
past the cleft of skin
he had wandered into.

And there
somewhere south of Eve
when someone
peeling back
the torso of night
handed out fishes & rolls
to saints & whores
who had smiled
knowing the others' vices
knowing who would
really be needed
if it ever
came down to it.

Number 7

He lived alone in Number 7, his wife well gone. He slept in the afternoons, woke in the middle of the night and went to the kitchen to make a cup of tea and smoke a cigarette. He only smoked one a day and looked forward to it.

Number 7 was the worse house in the street.

He often sat in a plastic chair on the front porch and watched the kids coming home from school. He rode a green scooter, a lime-green scooter, the type that has trouble getting up steep hills.

Sometimes he played old cassettes and cried. When it became too much, he went into the garden and pruned the plumbago into a perfect sphere. Pruned the hedge into a triangle.

They use to picnic on the lawn. Spread a blanket on hot nights and eat chicken and drank red wine.

The body and blood. Amen.

Spelling

Dear Mr Maroney, you probably don't remember me, unless through my absences. At a recent reunion, we decided to form a group to talk out our schooldays. Teachers who were a distinct influence. Marked our way through life. Your name came up first – quite vehemently, in fact – especially when we recalled how you lined us around the wall for spelling. A bit like being on the other side of the firing squad. You using words like bullets. Answers quick and unfaltering, or else to the back of the line. At the end of the lesson, the last five boys were strapped. Laurie O'Neill – the redhead you called Blue – still can't line up in queues unless there are five people behind him. He's had a life of being abused or shoved to the back. Mick Taylor never had a stuttering problem till he couldn't get out sustenance right before the bell. The perfect student who got strapped. You told him it would keep him on his toes. Den Rand hates his kids asking him how to spell a word. You kept the strap on the desk or sometimes in your back pocket. It looked like a small black tail and with your wrinkled face gave us one of your nicknames, monkey Maroney. Chris Hill still has an unnatural aversion to the lesser apes and some of the smaller tailed primates. But it was the threat of your special strap – Jumbo, you called it, speaking affectionately of it as if it was your cat or dog. The way you soaked it in oil once a month to give it flex or polished it with boot polish to keep its shine. It was hidden in a back cupboard that you kept locked. We could only remember you using it once (on Phil Ray – typical) but the fear of it kept us wary. Sam Locke had to sit next to it at the back of the room. We were seated from one at the front to forty-eight at the back dependent on our tests. His analyst attributes most of his neuroses to the palpable presence of Jumbo – alive and breathing, oiled like a bodybuilder in the darkness of the cupboard. You took most of our meeting, you and your spelling line and the oiled Jumbo. Steve Gatt reminded us how you would trick us into learning our lists by asking the compound word in the list or the word that rhymes with. He said you had little effect on him and had come along for the alcohol but he did say that he remembers you when he hears the compound word that double rhymes with pass and role.

Cigarette

Branislav returned to the beachfront seven days after the old man had fell with a perfect bullet to the right side of his head. A forty-five degree angle to the left of the right ear. Angles. He had learnt so much about angles as a marksman. So much depended on angles. As a child learning English as a second language, he had mixed up angles and angels, and as he grew older heard the adage of the angel and devil on each shoulder, but knew they were both angels.

He had felt the weight of each of them on his shoulders during the war, and after last week's shooting, he had barely the strength to carry them both home on his back.

He had come at dusk to this place above the ocean to debate with himself, hoping something would blow in from offshore to reassure him. He didn't know if he would make it home.

After the war, he had taken up serious walking. For hours at a time, just to exhaust himself. It was always better along the edge of water and since being in Australia the long white beaches, dreamlike and hallucinogenic, helped to exile his demons, dragging them out to drown. Watching the bubbles subside as he held them under. It was the walking, and its steady pace that might cure him eventually. Arms moving up and down, to balance, to continually correct the imbalance, that made his hold on earth so fragile.

But that evening he didn't know who would be dragged out and drowned.

He leaned his head back and closed his eyes. He would have liked to howl like those wolves in the mountains of home that he listened to as a boy. As a child, he never thought the sound of the wolves were sad; it was more a release, a cathartic outpouring.

He had believed himself to be an ethical man, but he laughed now when he tried to think of his life. We are all liars, then knew it a sophist trick. Nevertheless, he believed that he never did the man harm. The old man had wanted this ending to his life and he had simply fulfilled an agreement between adults. Did he have the right? Yes, he did, and though not totally convinced, it would have to do for now, and he forestalled the walk along the beach and turned and started home.

It was not long, a kilometre or two, before he felt as if he was going to collapse. He just wanted to sleep. He could crawl up now and sleep on the side of the road, he had slept in a thousand worse places, but there was now the noisy exhaust of an old car driving up the road.

Branislav walked on till he had to lean against a wall. He was right next to a gate, so he opened it and went in, hoping that there was somewhere he could hide for the night. A sheltered wall, a patch of grass, ideally a backshed. All places he had crawled to and lay in another life.

He walked around the house but the lights had come on. He didn't want trouble, and he knew how easily it was for him to injure others. Then the back door opened, and an old woman in a dressing gown speaking to the intruder. He didn't make out all the words, but it sounded like she wanted a cigarette. He was about to offer her a roll-your-own, but knew his appearance would scare her, so he stayed quiet, waiting for her to go back to bed so he could leave.

Approaching Zero

There are the same number of bones
in the human body as nations on earth,
the same number of border wars
as the prophet's days in the desert.
Each bone a nation, body a world.
Algebra, from the Arabic, the repair
of broken bones, sure-footing an equation.
You can imagine those first fights, a stone
lifted in biblical anger bone-breaking
a brother. Calculus, Latin for small stone,
a thousand years to be worn smooth.
The number of natural elements,
the same as the days of summer.
Geometry is far more practical:
to measure the earth, to plot out property,
anticipating later economics.
For ownership you just need simple
arithmetic: to divide and subtract.
The bottom fifty per cent have the same
wealth as twenty-six billionaires.

There are the same number of black deaths
in custody in Australia as the year Attila
became King of the Huns. *Each broken bone.*
Trigonometry, a study of angles
and sides, chords in a circle, the chant
of Circe. The same number of languages
lost as the sixteenth Fibonacci.

Zero is not the same as nothing,
taken centuries to discover, though
it is for half the world. The word hungry
and hollow. Extinction: when a species
reaches zero. The same number of
extinctions in a year as years since
Brahmagupta first explained zero.
In algebra you cannot divide by zero,
we need calculus and its curved line
that speaks only of approaching zero,
the asymptote that never quite touches.